I0626263

OLD YULE LOG FIRES

A MINNESOTA LAKES CHRISTMAS ROMANCE

ROSE MARIE MEUWISSEN

A CHRISTMAS ROMANCE

Old Yule log Fires

by

Rose Marie Meuwissen

Old Yule Log Fires
Digital/Print Edition
Copyright 2020 by Rose Marie Meuwissen
https://www.rosemariemeuwissen.com

Old Yule Log Fires is a work of fiction. Names, characters, and incidents depicted in this book are products of the author's imagination or are used fictitiously. Any resemblance to actual events, locales, organizations, or persons, living or dead, is entirely coincidental and beyond the intent of the author or the publisher. No part of this book may be reproduced or transmitted in any form or by any means, electronic or mechanical, including photocopying, recording, or by any information storage and retrieval system, without permission in writing from the publisher.

NO GHOSTWRITERS WERE USED IN THE CREATION OF THIS BOOK. THIS WORK OF FICTION IS 100% THE ORIGINAL WORK OF ROSE MARIE MEUWISSEN.

Print ISBN: 978-0-9903788-9-1
Published in the United States of America
Nordic Publishing
Edited by Leanore Elliot
Cover Design by Rose Marie Meuwissen

nordic
PUBLISHING

❀ Created with Vellum

To the Old Log Theater in Excelsior where I enjoyed the opportunity to watch the play, Snow White and the Seven Vikings, and the beautiful city of Wayzata, on the shores of Lake Minnetonka, decorated in its Christmas finery, all of which inspired this Christmas story.

A MINNESOTA LAKES ROMANCE
NOVELETTE

Lake Minnetonka

OLD YULE LOG FIRES

The Old Log theater manager, Tara, has a Christmas crisis. Ty, her high school sweetheart, now a Hollywood heartthrob, is back and starring in the big holiday show. It's been ten years since they'd even spoken to each other. Meeting him again, wasn't going to be easy.

Even though Ty met his fair share of women in LA, he'd never forgotten his first love. But, when he'd left her heartbroken, returning to Minnesota wasn't in his plans. Now that he was ready to settle down and start a family, the only woman he'd even consider proposing to, probably wasn't even speaking to him.

Sparks will fly, but can the smoldering ashes from an old log catch fire and allow the flames of true love to burn once again?

A MINNESOTA LAKES CHRISTMAS ROMANCE

MINNESOTA

Land of 10,000 Lakes

A MINNESOTA CHRISTMAS ROMANCE

Old Yule Log Fires

by

Rose Marie Meuwissen

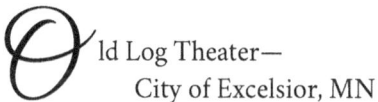

ld Log Theater—
City of Excelsior, MN

"I said no interruptions, Molly. I have to get these ads in by ten or we won't have any advertisements for this last minute *Christmas Time Again* show, that for some reason, Mike thought we could fit in!" Tara Knutsen glanced up from the file on her desk and leaned back in her chair with exasperation reeling from every inch of her trim body.

"I know, I'm sorry, but he's here." Molly fidgeted her fingers into an iron fist in front of her body while she waited for a response.

"And just who is here, that has you in such a tizzy?" Tara stared at Molly, wondering if the whole world was against her getting this ad submitted this morning.

"The lead actor for the Christmas show."

"Now? He wasn't supposed to be here until tomorrow night!"

"Yes, but he's here now. What should I tell him?" Molly shuffled her feet back and forth in a rocking motion.

"Well, I can't talk to him right now. If I don't run these ads, there won't be anyone at his little impromptu last minute show." Tara spun her chair around to face the window to see the snow coming down gently. For now, anyway. A snowstorm was forecast for later in the afternoon, and probably why he flew in early. *What else could possibly go wrong today?* "Tell him I'm on a conference call and will be out to meet him in about thirty minutes."

"Sure. What if he doesn't want to wait? After all, he's a big movie star and they can be kind of –you know what I mean."

"Take him on a tour of the theater and by the time you're done, I should be ready." Tara made a shooing motion with her hand for Molly to leave and refocused on the file she'd attempted to open only minutes before.

She hadn't even had time to read it yet, much less get the advertising ready. Mike plopped the file on her desk a few minutes after she'd arrived in the office this morning. Just who was this guy that he had the nerve to show up a day early and expect her to be available? She opened the file and flipped through the papers to the back sheet to find his name and photo.

When she looked at the man's extremely photogenic face in the picture, her breath caught in her chest. His chiseled features, strong jawline and jet black hair brought back memories she'd buried long ago. She didn't have to look at the name to know who he was, she would know those dark brown eyes anywhere. They were the eyes that haunted her dreams for the past ten years. She could feel her blood pressure rising at the thought of seeing him again. He'd changed his name, she knew this much, but she hadn't cared to find out what it was. Now she knew. Tyler Callaghan was now Ty Logan. And apparently, he waited just beyond her door. She felt literally sick. *Maybe I could plead a migraine and leave before they came back?*

Tara had little choice at this point. She needed to do her job and face her worst nightmare. Hell, they were *only* high school sweethearts. Never got engaged. They were only kids back then and had no idea where their lives were going or where they'd end up. Unfortunately, she'd assumed they had a future together. He'd been her first love and she thought he loved her, too. Then he'd left and never contacted her again. Obviously, he hadn't felt the same about her. She'd hoped to never see him again, but deep down she'd believed this day would come.

The advertising was taken care of and it had only been twenty minutes. Just enough time to google *Ty Logan. Did that mean a person was famous if they had their own Wikipedia page?* Well, he did have one and it said he'd done some B movies and been in a few TV shows. She did feel a little surprised to find out he'd been singing for fun at some events, recently. Apparently, she wasn't the only one who liked to listen to him sing. *After living in LA all these years, why would he want to come to Minnesota and sing at the Old Log Theater on Lake Minnetonka?*

Being an adult, Tara knew she would live through coming face-to-face with her ex-boyfriend. But damn it, she was still pissed as hell at him, and definitely didn't have to like it. Perhaps she could act like she didn't know who he was? Yeah, maybe she could give that a try.

After a few deep cleansing breaths, she rose slowly from her chair and walked to the door. Another deep breath and she opened it. For a moment, she hesitated, when she saw him turn her way.

Briefly, an elated expression crossed his tan chiseled face. Yes, this was one very hot, sexy man. Quickly, he walked towards her extending his hand to shake hers. Now with a much more serious expression, his eyes locked on hers as if he was trying to see deep into her soul. "TJ Sandstrom," Tyler stated and waited patiently for her response.

Of course, he would use her nick name and maiden name. "Tara Knutsen," she corrected him and extended her hand to meet his, but as soon as their hands touched, it became overwhelmingly apparent the shocking chemistry they'd experienced as teenagers was still there. "Mr. Logan, welcome to the Old Log Theater. I hope you enjoyed your tour and Molly filled you in on what will be happening for your show."

"Yes, she did. Thank you." Tyler released her hand slowly.

"Please let the stage manager, Tom, know if you need anything. If you are all set then, I need to get back to work." She waited for his nod to say she could end this meeting, but it was slow coming.

"I'm good, for now, but can we discuss some small details concerning the show and its advertising over dinner? Say tonight, if you're free?"

"I have plans for tonight." Her nerves were raw. *How dare he ask me to dinner at the last minute and expect me to be free?*

Mike, the theater manager, walked over to where they were standing just in time to hear her decline Tyler's invitation. "Mr. Logan, I'm sure Tara will be happy to rearrange her schedule to accommodate your gracious offer for dinner." He gave her a stern look.

"Of course, Mr. Logan. If it's important and can't wait until tomorrow, I can cancel my plans."

"Lord Fletcher's at seven, then. Would you like me to pick you up or would you rather meet me there?" Tyler asked.

"I'll meet you there." With the inevitable settled, she turned and walked back to her office, shutting the door gently behind her, even though she very much wanted to slam it. *Hell yes, I'm driving myself!* It would only be a short quick dinner and then she was leaving.

Promptly at seven, Tara pulled up to Lord Fletcher's restaurant and used the valet service. She got out of her SUV and with her manicured nails, she nervously straightened her form fitting low cut black dress which fell mid-thigh. Then she pulled her long black wool coat closed. Her goal, of course, was to show him what he'd passed up for Hollywood.

CHAPTER 2

*T*yler waited patiently in the lobby. As soon as he saw her long legs in knee high black leather boots with her hot sexy body in a short, skin tight dress walking provocatively through the doors, he knew it was his TJ. He could sense the unease she'd felt at seeing him again and she had every right to be mad. His heart had skipped a beat when he first saw her today.

Her long blonde hair fell gently past her shoulders and her big blue eyes were like pools of clear blue lake water totally mesmerizing him. She'd appeared to be even more beautiful now than when they were in high school, if that was even possible. He'd been a fool back then. Leaving her behind had always been his biggest regret. He loved her and no one else ever came close to making him feel the things she did. If it were possible to correct a mistake he'd made ten years ago, he intended to do it.

He immediately walked over to greet her. Unexpectedly, he leaned in and pulled her towards him for a kiss, wrapping her tightly in his arms. To his surprise, she responded by kissing him back. Pissing her off wasn't what he had in mind though, so he reluctantly stopped. He smiled at her and motioned towards the door. "I'm sure our table is ready."

Turning away quickly, Tara entered the restaurant.

"Do you have a reservation, sir?" the hostess asked.

"Yes, Ty Logan," he quickly answered.

"Right this way." The hostess escorted them to a deep burgundy rounded booth with high leather-like backs providing some privacy.

"Please bring us a bottle of your house wine," Tyler stated.

"Certainly." The hostess left swiftly, seeming to be eager to do his bidding.

"I'm grateful you accepted my offer for dinner." Tyler intently watched Tara's face, waiting for her reaction, while the hostess returned with their wine and filled each glass.

Tara twisted her glass, then took a sip as she stared at him intently. "I didn't really have a choice."

"Everyone always has choices. We can all only hope we make the right ones."

"Apparently, you did," Tara retorted implying what they both knew was his decision to leave years ago.

"Is that the way it appears to you?" He never felt nervous but talking to her tonight was one of the hardest things he'd ever done. This was the woman he loved and he'd broken her heart years ago.

"Yes." That was all she said, but her eyes were a force to be reckoned with almost as if she was daring him to deny it.

"It may look that way to you, but I'm not sure." He'd wanted to go to Hollywood and become a famous actor. Unfortunately, he'd felt he needed to do it alone, so here they were basically strangers after all these years, trying to get past the pain and hurt his decision had caused.

"Is that why we're here? Did you expect to find me married with children? A fat, dumpy housewife? Is that what you were hoping?"

"Actually, I was hoping to find you still as beautiful as ever."

"Really? And just sitting around waiting for you to return?"

"Well, I knew that would be asking a lot, but yes something like that. And may I say, for the record, you are even more beautiful today than when I last saw you."

Thank heavens the waitress appeared at the table just in the nick of time. After placing their orders, they both sat staring at each other.

Finally, Tara broke the silence, "I think we need to change the subject to work related. I looked over the plans for your show and was surprised to learn you would be doing a musical Christmas show."

"You, of all people know how much I like to sing. Even after achieving success as an actor, what I really wanted to do was sing. Only after I became somewhat well-known, would they allow me to perform songs on the shows. So doing this live show is really something I've wanted to do for a long time."

"I always loved to listen to your singing."

"I figured if anyone would let me sing on their stage, it would be in my home town. So I had my agent contact the Old Log Theater and here we are."

"I'm sure it will be a great show."

The waitress brought their bread and salads as they discussed the show. Lord Fletcher's was known for their steaks and seafood and once the dinner plates were served, it left no doubt as to why.

After they'd finished their dinners, he requested a dessert menu. "We'll take the Mud Pie," Tyler informed the waitress without asking Tara's opinion. He wondered if she remembered this was the same place they went to dinner for Prom.

Mud Pie was what they had for dessert. "I wonder if it's still as good as it was?"

Tara stared at him. "I guess we'll find out. The last time I was here was for Prom with you."

As soon as dessert was done, Tara got up to leave but he insisted on walking her out. "Thanks for dinner," she said as he moved closer to her. Out of the corner of her eye, she could see other women, even those with men, ogling Tyler. She knew he was famous but she didn't need anyone taking pictures of her with him and printing it in the newspapers or tabloids. He was her past and that would be the way it would stay. Heck, women were probably throwing themselves at him all the time. He definitely wasn't going to be kissing her again, either. So as soon as the car pulled up, she walked around, got in and left him standing there without another word.

While she drove away, she could see him still standing at the curb. She had to admit, it wasn't so much that he might try to kiss her again, it was that she just didn't trust herself not to kiss him back.

Why did he have to come back now? And to my theater? She truly never expected to see him again. It had taken five years to get over him and during those years, she'd really thought he would come back. But he didn't. After meeting Steve, she tried desperately to fall in love with him and even thought she had. So she married him, hoping then she would experience the same feelings for him that she'd felt for Tyler. Sadly, it hadn't happened. Three years later, the divorce papers were filed.

When she looked Tyler up on the internet, it showed pictures of him with many different women. They were all gorgeous and obviously, he could have any of them. *Why was he really in Minneapolis?* She didn't have a clue but she needed to stay as far away from him as possible because the only thing that could come out of this situation was for her to get her heart broken again.

The next week went by quickly and she hadn't seen him too much since he was rehearsing the show like a mad man to get it perfect. She tried to avoid being where he might be as much as possible. Saturday, December 12-tomorrow-the first show would open and it would run for ten days with the last show just two days before Christmas Eve.

Every time she walked by the theater and he was singing, she stopped to listen. He'd always been a great singer, in fact probably a better singer than actor. Of course, she wasn't going to tell him that. Needless to say, it was going to be a spectacular show and they were sold out for all ten nights.

Evergreen boughs hung from the ceilings, pine wreaths decorated the walls along with red and white Christmas lights. In the main foyer, a nine foot spruce Christmas tree stood with red and gold ribbon bows, white lights and ornaments hand made by the Old Log employees. Mistletoe hung over the main door, only it was hidden-not noticeable among the other greenery and flowers-so unless you were extremely observant or actually looking for it, you wouldn't see it.

It had been snowing again and she decided to head out early to do some Christmas shopping when accidentally she ran right smack into Tyler's chest as she came around the corner.

"Easy does it, sweetheart." His lips were inches from her cheek.

"So sorry," she said and quickly backed away. When their bodies touched briefly, she felt sparks like she'd never felt before. She couldn't help wondering what it would be like to feel his hard body pressed against hers while having wild crazy sex.

"Where are you off to in such a hurry?"

"Oh, just wanted to get in some Christmas shopping before the weather gets too bad."

"Living in California, you forget about the dangers of driving in snow."

"It'll probably come back to you."

"Care if I tag along with you? I'd love to have some company for dinner. Never liked eating dinner alone."

"Tyler, what do you want from me?"

"Ever wonder what would've happen if I'd stayed?"

"You didn't, so it doesn't matter, does it?"

"That depends."

"On what?" She was getting agitated now. Of course, she wondered, why wouldn't she?

The rest of the show crew came walking down the hall towards them, laughing and talking.

"I'll buy," Tyler offered, deliberately avoiding her question and gave her his sexy grin that usually had women falling at his feet.

"Fine, let's go," Tara finally said as she didn't want to deal with the rest of show crew.

CHAPTER 3

*H*e followed her out to the parking lot. The snow had been falling steadily all afternoon, leaving about two inches of fresh snow on the ground.

"Where's your car?" she asked.

Tyler pointed to a shiny new Chevy Suburban still sporting dealer plates.

They continued walking to her SUV, a Christmas red Ford Escape. He immediately picked up the snow scraper from the backseat and brushed it off while she started the engine. Minutes later, she drove to downtown Wayzata and parked. It was dark now and the streets were lined with Christmas lights and decorations.

She loved Christmas! And this was why. Everything was decorated so beautifully.

Tyler got out, came around to her side to open the door and helped her out.

It'd been years since she'd spent any time around Christmas with a man. Unfortunately, only a temporary situation though, and she needed to keep telling herself this because he would be leaving again. Maybe for a little while she could just enjoy her time with him. As a friend. *Hell, who am I kidding?* They were more than friends back then. She'd given him her virginity long ago on Prom night. The chemistry between them had been strong then and it hadn't died out even one bit—like a smoldering old log fire that hadn't gone out completely. The attraction they felt could easily be fanned into a brilliant burning flame once again.

Together, they strolled down the sidewalk in front of the Main Street storefronts. She went in the shops where she saw interesting items in the windows and he followed with a smile.

"I thought guys hated to go shopping."

"I'm thoroughly enjoying this. Interesting, quaint little shops. I'm glad they've kept this area alive and vibrant all these years. It must be a nice place to live."

"They've done a good job, I agree. I especially like to come here at least one time before Christmas."

While they walked along Main Street, they ultimately ended up at what once was *Sunsetter's* for many years, now under new management and called *Cove*. Large wreaths with large round red glass bulbs adorned the front doors.

"The new restaurant looks welcoming and warm. Want to have dinner, here?" he asked.

"I don't—know," she replied eyeing the doors.

"It's only dinner. You must be hungry."

"Okay." After all, she'd only had a snack for lunch. How difficult could it be to have dinner with him, again? In fact, she might actually enjoy it. So far, he'd been good company and he *had* initially invited her to dinner.

Apparently, someone on the staff recognized him, because they got the best table in the place, on second floor directly overlooking Lake Minnetonka and Main Street. Once seated at their secluded table, they weren't bothered by other people dining who might have realized a celebrity dined in their midst.

They ordered the special, Salmon, and opted for just coffee since it was still snowing and the roads would be slippery.

"I have to say, I miss this little town. So tell me what you've been doing all these years?"

"Going to college, getting a job, etc. The usual stuff."

"Did you leave out getting married?"

"I would think that was obvious by my last name."

"I don't see a ring."

"Divorced. It didn't work out. How about you?"

"Never took the big step. Didn't think it would work out with anyone I'd met."

The rest of the conversation centered around small talk and about how Wayzata had changed over the last years. After finishing their meals, they managed to make it out of the restaurant without being stopped by any over-anxious fans. The snow seemed to be coming down pretty good by then, but she made it safely back to the Old Log Theater to drop him off.

It was nearly ten when she pulled up beside his SUV, now covered in snow.

Tyler pulled out his key and pressed the auto start button. "Thank you for letting me tag along for your Christmas shopping night in Wayzata and for rescuing me from having to eat dinner alone."

"I had a nice time. Thanks for the dinner and the company."

Tyler jumped out, and opened the door to pull out a snow brush and begin the task of clearing off his vehicle for the drive home as she drove away.

CHAPTER 4

*O*pening night was a huge success, with rave reviews being printed in the local newspapers. Tara had sat in the back row of the theater to watch the show, telling herself it was part of her job, but she really wanted to see the show. The man was good, she would give him that and damn good looking, too. Even though he'd only been back a short time, she could tell she was falling in love with him all over again. *That is if I ever stopped loving him.*

The ten days of the show went by quickly and each night, they had a full house. Once it ended its run, he would most likely be leaving and heading back to Los Angeles. Every time she saw him at the theater, he smiled at her and he always acted gracious and kind to the staff. Never once had she seen him act haughtily towards anyone. *Could he still be the nice guy I once knew and fell in love with? Do I dare tell him I still have feelings for him?*

Finally, the last day of the show arrived and Molly walked into Tara's office carrying a flyer. "There's a party at Ty's tomorrow night for the staff," she said and handed one to

Tara. "Everyone's excited to go see his house. You're going to go, aren't you?"

"Of course, if everyone is going. I wasn't aware he had a house in Minnesota. Where is it?"

"Someone said it's a huge mansion on Lake Minnetonka. Gotta hand all these out, so I'll be back in a little bit."

Tara's SUV turned up the long winding driveway to Tyler's place. The large brick house loomed in front of her. Every window glowed from a single candle and the house had been completely trimmed with white lights. She still couldn't believe this was Tyler's. *Why would he buy a mansion on the lake when he lived in California?*

Getting out of her SUV, she heard, *Jingle Bell Rock*, emanating from the open door as several people entered the beautifully decorated house. Through the large front window, a Christmas tree, ornately adorned and totally aglow from the multitude of white lights, could be seen. Inside, people dressed in their holiday finery conversed and laughed while enjoying each other's company.

When she reached the door to knock politely before letting herself in, it opened and Tyler greeted her with his sexy and stunning smile. "Tara. Glad you made it." He stepped aside, so she could enter. While she unhooked her coat, he waited to take it. "Let me put your coat away, for you."

She waited patiently until he returned while taking in the center staircase adorned in evergreen boughs and red ribbons. *Blue Christmas* played in the background. It seemed like such a happy place and it gave her a comfortable feeling. She smiled at him when he returned and took his arm as he extended it to her.

"Let me show you my new house."

He showed her each room on the main floor and then proceeded upstairs to show her the master bedroom. Molly had been right, this was definitely a mansion! The bedroom looked enormous, complete with a sitting room, exercise room, massive his and her closets and a large veranda outside of the triple patio doors. She didn't know what to say. "It's absolutely gorgeous. Who will you be sharing this bed with?" she asked pointing to the large king bed. As soon as she asked, she wished she hadn't.

"That depends on what happens here."

Sheer shock overtook her. "What does that mean? You want to have sex here and right now?"

"Not exactly, but by no means would I turn down a chance to make love to you again." He laughed softly.

"What do you want from me, Tyler?" She had no idea what might be happening or was about to happen.

He moved closer and wrapped his arms around her. "I never stopped loving you, Tara. I would like a second chance for us." His voice lowered and his lips moved closer to hers until they touched her waiting lips. This time, he kissed her not holding anything back—like he never wanted to let her go again.

Her resolve to stay though guarded, melted away and she kissed him back with every ounce of her being.

Tara thought about the huge inviting bed behind them, but knew she wouldn't be using it tonight. Reluctantly, she moved slightly away from him to end the kiss, even though every inch of her body wanted him inside her. "This is happening too fast, Tyler," she whispered to him. "I was mad at you for way too many years, so I couldn't even move on. I waited for five years, hoping you would come back for me, but you didn't."

"But after that, you got married, right? So you did move on."

"I tried to, regrettably I never loved him the way I loved you. I had to let him go, so he'd have a chance to find a love like you and I had. Unfortunately, I don't think I ever stopped loving you, which left me unable to love anyone else."

"I never married because I never had feelings for anyone else that even came close to what I'd felt for you. That's why I came back home. For you."

"And you bought this house, why? Are you staying in Minnesota?"

"I want to take some time off from Hollywood and get back to my roots. Hopefully, get married and start a family. With you."

Tara backed away, running her fingers through her long blonde hair. "This is really a lot to take in, Tyler. I've waited for ten years to hear you say those words, but now that you finally have, I don't know what to say."

"You don't have to give me an answer tonight. I've been thinking about this for the past year before making my decision to come back home and contact you. It was sheer coincidence that you were working at the Old Log. Or maybe it was fate. Our fate."

"Tyler, this is ten years later. We are older and we are different people now than we were before. Getting back together may be a dream come true for us, but we need to take some time and really get to know each other again."

"I've got time. I'm willing to go slow if that's what you want. I would just like a chance to find out if we still love each other enough to make it work. The Ordway offered me the lead in their new play, so I'll be staying here for a while."

"I need to take some time to think about this. It really has been quite a shock to hear this from you."

"I'm alright with that." He took her in his arms and softly kissed her cheek. Then brushed her lips gently with his, before kissing her once again. Slowly. Almost as though he was afraid it could be the last time he would have the opportunity.

She ended the kiss and laid her head on his shoulder. Not wanting to let go either.

"You do realize the chemistry between us is off the charts?" Tyler whispered in her ear.

"I do." Tara couldn't believe she was actually thinking maybe they should be moving to the bed only inches away.

"I have every confidence we can make it work and have a long and loving relationship."

"We probably should go mingle with your guests," Tara suggested, knowing this wasn't the proper time to take this any further.

"I'd rather not, but you're probably right, we should." He hesitated a moment, then took her hand in his and they descended the stairs to join the party.

The food he had catered in was top notch and she thoroughly enjoyed it while conversing with her co-workers. She watched Tyler out of the corner of her eye as he also mingled with the guests.

Finally, ten o'clock came and people were making their way to the door to head home. After all, tomorrow was still a work day for them even though the show had ended.

Tara ended up being the last to leave, but not because she planned it that way. She'd already remotely started her car and had it warming up, when she realized everyone was gone and only she and Tyler were left standing in the foyer.

Tyler brought her coat out and helped her put it on. She suddenly felt tempted to ascend those stairs with him and use that welcoming king bed where they could become reacquainted with each other, but it was late. She had no doubt in her mind that every inch of her being wanted to be with him, but she really needed to think about this with a clear head and in the light of day.

"Would you like to spend Christmas Eve together?" Tyler asked. "We could make dinner here."

"I go to church on Christmas Eve, would you like to join me?"

"I'd love to. You still go to Grace Lutheran?"

"Yes. I can pick you up at five-thirty. Afterwards, we can cook dinner." Tara felt excited at the idea.

"Great. I'll go grocery shopping tomorrow morning."

Tara leaned into him and gave him a quick kiss. Then turned and walked to her car. She could feel his eyes on her back, watching her walk away from him and she smiled.

CHAPTER 5

On Christmas Eve morning, Tara woke to bright sunlight streaming in through the small opening at the bottom of her curtained window.

She hadn't been this happy at Christmas time in years. It'd been lonely spending it by herself. On Christmas Day, she always went to her parent's house for dinner along with her sister, brother and their spouses. Neither had children yet, so it was strictly an adult's Christmas. She hadn't allowed herself to even think about what it would be like with children or a husband since there wasn't anyone she'd been serious about since the divorce. Did she dare think about it now? Was he being honest about his intentions? Should she take the chance to find out? Hell, if she knew whether it would work out or not. The only thing she had to lose by trying would be her heart. Again.

After showering and dressing, she headed out to find the perfect present for Tyler. She didn't know of course, if he would be getting one for her, but she wanted to be prepared. *But what did you get someone who could probably buy whatever they wanted?*

Nothing came to mind, until she walked into a store called *Christmas Time Again* at the Ridgedale Mall. She felt drawn to a snow globe portraying a singer on a stage with the words, *Christmas Time Again*, on the outside of the pedestal it rested on—the perfect gift.

She hurriedly grabbed a bite to eat at the coffee shop and headed home to change clothes.

Dressed in a Christmas red dress that snugly clung to every curve of her body as it came to just above the knee, she paired it with a pair of black leather pumps. She drove to pick up Tyler. When she arrived, his house was aglow from the multitudes of white Christmas lights.

He immediately came out and got in the car as if he'd been watching closely for her to arrive.

At the church, the parking lot looked nearly full, but she managed to find a spot in the back. They walked in and took their seats just minutes before the service started. The annual Christmas service, featured children reading segments of the Christmas story and the congregation singing the much loved and well known Christmas hymns.

It warmed her heart to hear Tyler singing loudly and with enthusiasm along with the congregation and herself. Attending church together was something she wanted for her future family and Tyler could possibly end up being part of that. It was a good sign!

Some of the older members recognized Tyler and came over to say hello. The older people who were their parent's ages remembered him as a child. Others she felt sure knew who he was now, but they were still gracious while allowing him his privacy and welcomed him to the church.

When they arrived back at his house, he opened the garage so she could pull her car inside since it had begun snowing again. She reached into the backseat and grabbed the bag she'd brought along containing a change of clothes and Tyler's present.

"I bought a couple of steaks to grill, salad greens, baking potatoes, and an assorted tray of Christmas cookies from the bakery. It happens to include your favorite ones, the peanut butter cookies with the Hershey kisses. I think they're called Peanut Butter Kiss cookies. And of course, wine."

While the steaks were grilling on the back patio with a low flame, they walked the short distance down to the lake. It looked frozen of course, with at least a thin coating of ice on top and covered in snow. The view was breathtaking as they could see all the houses across from them on the opposite bay, glowing from their Christmas lights. It was lightly snowing, surrounding them in an immensely romantic aura.

"It's beautiful out here," she said gazing out over the lake while sipping the hot mint cocoa in her mug.

"I'm glad you like it. Remember when we used to go to the public beach and wonder about all the people in the big houses on the lake?"

"Yes, I remember."

"Now, we're those people." He chuckled. "And if we don't want burnt steaks, we better go rescue our dinner."

"Can't wait to try those cookies, either. They are still my favorite."

Sitting on the couch after dinner, with only the Christmas tree lights to brighten the room, they watched the fire burning while enjoying Christmas music. It just so happened to be a CD Tyler had recorded containing his versions of the old Christmas favorites.

He'd done a great job and she would have to get a copy for herself.

He reached over to put his arm around her shoulder and pull her closer to him. She obliged and laid her head on his shoulder.

"Did you have time to think about what we talked about yesterday?"

"Yes."

"And…" Tyler paused waiting for her answer.

"I don't want to have my heart broken again." Tara looked down afraid to meet his eyes.

"I can't make any promises except that I love you and I will give 100% to make our relationship work. I want to marry *you* and start a family." He gently tipped her chin up and kissed her, then suddenly ended the kiss.

"I have a present for you." He reached under the tree and handed her a small box.

Why was it sometimes small boxes were scary to open? What could he have gotten her? Tara slowly unwrapped it and opened the box. Shock rippled through her as she removed a ring from the box. A magnificent large—at least two carats—diamond ring. "I don't understand," she said, her voice almost a whisper.

"I know it's kind of a strange proposal, but I love you and always have. I want to marry you and make up for the last ten years of my stupidity by showing you each and every day how much I've missed you."

"But we have a lot of catching up to do, before we can have a serious talk about marriage."

"I agree, but I want you to know I am serious about getting married and us. You can hold on to it until you feel comfortable wearing it."

"And if I don't and this doesn't work out, then what?"

"You can do whatever you want with it. It's yours."

She must be crazy to even be considering his proposal, but she was thinking about it. Being together with Tyler was something she'd wanted for so long, why shouldn't she at least consider it? Slowly, she slid the ring on her finger. "I got something for you," she said and got up to get his present from her bag. She handed it to him.

He eagerly opened it and took out the snow globe. When he saw the inscription—*Christmas Time Again*—he smiled. "It will remind me of coming back to Minnesota. I love it! It's the perfect gift. Thank you." He then glanced at the ring on her finger waiting for her answer.

"I have wanted this moment to happen, forever it seems like, and now that it has, I don't see any reason to turn down your offer. Yes, I will give us a second chance."

He kissed her, a kiss that escalated both of their body temperatures. From smoldering ashes, a blazing flame rose up between them. Pausing momentarily, they both looked toward the staircase. Tyler got up and took her hand. Above the landing of the staircase, hung Christmas mistletoe. He stopped and turned her into his arms. Their lips met. Lighting a fire deep into their souls.

"Merry Christmas, Tyler," she whispered against his lips.

"Merry Christmas, Tara," he replied, his voice raspy.

She'd waited ten years to have this chance and she wasn't about to waste any more time. Tara took his hand and they walked up the dimly lit, romantic staircase. Their second chance at love would begin tonight.

From smoldering ashes came an old log's brightly burning flame.

Peanut Butter Kiss Cookies
Christmas Cookies

Ingredients

- ½ cup butter
- 1/3 cup peanut butter
- ½ cup sugar
- ½ cup brown sugar
- 1 egg
- 1 tsp vanilla
- 2 Tbsp milk
- 1 ¾ cup flour
- 1 tsp baking soda
- ½ tsp salt
- 1 bag of Hershey's Kisses (Milk Chocolate)

Directions

- Mix softened butter, peanut butter, sugar and brown sugar in bowl.
- Add egg, vanilla and milk. Stir until batter is smooth.
- Mix in flour, baking soda and salt. Dough should be firm. Chill for 1-2 hours.
- Roll into ½ inch balls and roll in sugar. Place on cookie sheet.
- Bake 8 minutes at 375 degrees.
- Take cookie sheet out of oven and place an unwrapped Hershey's Kiss on each cookie, pressing down slightly.
- Bake 2-5 minutes longer and then remove from oven.

ABOUT THE AUTHOR

Rose Marie Meuwissen, a first-generation Norwegian American born and raised in Minnesota, always tries to incorporate her Norwegian heritage into her writing. After receiving a BA in Marketing from Concordia University, a Masters in Creative Writing from Hamline University soon followed. Minnesota is still where she calls home.

She has traveled around the world, including Scandinavia, but still has many places to see, enjoys attending Scandinavian events, writing conferences and is usually busy writing Minnesota Lakes Contemporary Romances, Viking Time Travel Romances or Norwegian Traditions Children's Books.

Visit her at www.rosemariemeuwissen.com or www. realnorwegianseatlutefisk.com.

NOVELS:

- *Taking Chances*—a contemporary romance novel set in Minnesota and Arizona.
- *Married by Saturday*—a contemporary romance novel set in Minnesota and Montana.
- *Looking for Mr. Right*—a contemporary internet dating romance novel set on Prior Lake in Minnesota—*Coming soon!*

NOVELLAS:

- *Annika—A Christmas Romance*—a contemporary romance set in Minnesota with a Nordic theme during the Christmas Holidays.
- *Skol! Viking Blonde Ale*—a contemporary romance set in Minnesota at an Autumn festival complete with a fortune teller, ale and Vikings!
- *Choosing to Live*—a Norwegian woman's journey during WWII to survive the Nazi Occupation of Norway—*Coming soon!*

MINNESOTA LAKES ROMANCE
NOVELETTES:

- *A Kiss Under the Northern Lights*—a Summer romance set in Ely, Minnesota on Big Lake.
- *Dancing in the Moonlight*—a Summer romance set in Malmo, Minnesota on Mille Lacs Lake.
- *Hot Summer Nights*—a Summer romance set in Prior Lake, Minnesota on Prior Lake.
- *Railroad Ties*—an Autumn romance set in Two Harbors, Minnesota on Lake Superior.
- *Blizzard of Love*—a Winter romance set in Lutsen, Minnesota on Lake Superior.
- *Nor-Way to Love*—a Spring romance set in Minneapolis, Minnesota on Lake Harriet.
- *Old Yule Log Fires*—a Christmas romance set in Excelsior, Minnesota on Lake Minnetonka.
- *A Date for Valentine's Day*—a Valentine romance set in Minnetonka Beach, Minnesota at the Lafayette Country Club on Lake Minnetonka.
- *Dance of Love*—a Fall Festival romance set at the Renaissance Fair in Shakopee, Minnesota.

CHILDREN'S BOOKS

REAL NORWEGIAN'S SERIES:

- *Real Norwegians Eat Lutefisk*—a Children's book about the tradition of Lutefisk presented in both English and Norwegian.
- *Real Norwegians Eat Rømmegrøt*—the second Children's book in the series about the tradition of Rømmegrøt presented in both English and Norwegian.
- *Real Norwegians Eat Lefse*—the third Children's book in the series about the tradition of Lefse presented in both English and Norwegian.
- *Real Norwegians Eat Krumkake*—the fourth Children's book in the series about the tradition of Krumkake presented in both English and Norwegian—*Coming next!*

MICRO-MINI NOVELETTE—COMING SOON!

Christmas Notes—a collection of Christmas prose poems to warm the heart during the Christmas season.

CONTINUE READING FOR A
PREVIEW OF:

ANNIKA—A CHRISTMAS ROMANCE

Betting on Paris Series

by

Rose Marie Meuwissen

ANNIKA—A CHRISTMAS ROMANCE

BETTING ON PARIS SERIES

Print Edition
Copyright 2020 by Rose Marie Meuwissen

Annika—A Christmas Romance is a work of fiction. Names, characters, and incidents depicted in this book are products of the author's imagination or are used fictitiously. Any resemblance to actual events, locales, organizations, or persons, living or dead, is entirely coincidental and beyond the intent of the author or the publisher. No part of this book may be reproduced or transmitted in any form or by any means, electronic or mechanical, including photocopying, recording, or by any information storage and retrieval system, without permission in writing from the publisher.

NO GHOSTWRITERS WERE USED IN THE CREATION OF THIS BOOK. This work of fiction is 100% the original work of Rose Marie Meuwissen.

ISBN 978-0-9903788-4-6
Published in the United States of America
Nordic Publishing LLC
Cover Design by Angie Speed

INTRODUCTION

Spend the holidays with Josie, Ryley, Emma, Alana, and Annika. Get ready for five weeks of romance with a new Christmas series brought to you by five exciting contemporary authors...

BETTING ON PARIS SERIES

Sometimes the best bet is the one you lose...

Five best friends. Five promises.

Each year in mid-August, the former college roommates meet up on a girls-only trip somewhere in the world. This year, it's Paris, the city of museums, art and romance. On the last night of their vacation, the girls engage in a serious talk about the sorry state of their love lives and collectively decide they are swearing off men. Instead, each woman is intent on pursuing her life's goal. Falling in love is the *last* thing on her mind!

This is ***Annika's*** story...

Owning Nordic Travel and Tours was a dream come true and Annika certainly didn't have time for romance. So why had she met the man of her dreams, now?

Tristan's Minnesota Events and Adventures Company for singles allowed him the ability to meet available women on a regular basis, so why would he be interested in her?

Annika had never mixed business with pleasure before and since Tristan would be booking tours through her company, there would be no romance. Now, she only had to convince her heart.

Find all the Betting on Paris novellas at Amazon!

Josie by Beth Gildersleeve
    Ryley by Donna Lovitz
    Emma by Angie Wilder
    Alana by Denise Devine
    Annika by Rose Marie Meuwissen

ANNIKA—CHAPTER 1

After driving around the parking ramp for what seemed like an eternity, Annika pulled her SUV into an empty spot and quickly unloaded two medium-sized plastic tubs onto her wheeled cart, then hurried toward the glassed-in elevator. Plopping her purse down on top of the tubs, she pressed the button for the main level while her eyes focused on her phone to check the time. *Only thirty minutes until the doors open for the Minneapolis Travel Expo at the convention center.*

She took a couple of calming breaths, trying to erase visions of the backed up freeway she'd just spent way too much time on during the morning rush hour traffic. Thank God, she lived and worked in the suburbs! Absolutely no way, would she put herself through that rat race every day to get to work. The door opened and she backed out of the elevator pulling the cart with her, but stopped abruptly when she felt a firm pressure on her back. The top bin went crashing to the floor sending her travel brochures into a very messy pile beside her cart. She turned around quickly to see what had stopped her dead in her tracks.

Piercing blue eyes and sandy blond hair focused on her.

Her face flushed in embarrassment. "I'm so sorry. I'm in a hurry and wasn't watching what or who was behind me as I backed out of the elevator."

He grinned at her, sliding his phone into his pocket and bent down to retrieve a handful of brochures. "I can't let you take all the blame. I was on my phone and not paying attention to my surroundings, either. Let me help you." He picked up more of the fallen brochures and placed them into the plastic container.

Annika picked up the remaining brochures setting them in the bin, carefully placing the cover over the top, pressing down until she heard the click signifying it was on tightly. "Thank you. I do have to run though." She turned and quickly walked into the main ballroom with her cart in tow after flashing the security guard her exhibitor nametag.

Thankfully, the booth had already been set up last night by her assistant, Holly, who would be arriving around noon after her prenatal doctor's appointment. Annika hadn't a clue what she would do without Holly for three months, maybe more, while she was out on maternity leave. The baby was due in October which was coming up way too soon.

They'd been late getting the newly designed brochures to the printer, only being able to pick them up yesterday afternoon which was why she'd been hauling them into the Expo this morning. She neatly arranged them on the table, and then sat down on the comfortably padded chair to reign in her emotions after her collision in the hallway. Typically, she didn't do things like that, but today she was off her normal routine after dealing with the traffic and rushing to get into the Expo before the event started and the doors opened. Well, she'd made it with a few minutes to spare. She picked up a bottle of water, left at the table for them by the Expo, and downed almost half of it, wanting to stay hydrated since she was about to do a lot of talking to potential customers and clients.

The guy she'd bumped into was definitely good looking, but she'd sworn off men for a year to concentrate on her business. Recently, on a trip to Paris with her best friends, Alana, Josie, Ryley and Emma, they'd all made a pact to focus on their jobs and to not let *any* men interfere with their career plans for a year. *Betting on Paris—No Men for a Year* was their pact slogan. Besides, her dream of owning her own travel tour company, Nordic Travel and Tours, had come true after the first of the year, when her boss, Dan Nystad, retired and sold it to her. Dan felt she was the best person to run the company and take it to the next step into the tech future of the twenty first century. He'd been a friend and mentor, teaching her everything about travel and tours for the past ten years of her career. She needed no distractions this year, especially, to make all the transitions needed to take her company into the new tech age, for which, it was sorely lacking.

At nine o'clock on the dot, the Expo's doors opened and people rushed in, eager to find all the freebies like pens, hats and bags, but hopefully there would be many who wanted to book tours and were serious about traveling in Minnesota and other places in the world, like Scandinavia, which was her specialty. Her booth would be giving away pens and brochures imprinted with photos of exciting cities and places to visit.

Soon, the aisles were full of people and many stopped at her booth to gaze at the breathtaking photos of the fjords of Norway on the promotional banners. Nothing could match their beauty. She handed out brochures and answered questions, trying to remember to take sips of water in between potential clients.

Holly arrived at noon carrying what appeared to be her lunch along with a large purse filled with necessities for the long day. "I made it." Holly sat down on the chair.

"I hope you didn't have to walk very far."

"No, I got a spot in the parking ramp, but at seven months pregnant any walking takes extra effort."

"Go ahead and eat your lunch and when you're done, I'll go get something from the food vendors."

Annika continued talking with the people walking through the Expo until Holly finished eating.

Holly stood up and walked to the counter. "I'm done so go ahead and get some lunch. Bet you didn't have any breakfast and are starving." She shooed Annika out of the booth.

Tristan watched the woman walk away. She definitely had poise and class, and appeared to be very professional. *Extremely attractive, too.* He was intrigued, but this was a work day and he was on a mission today. His Minnesota Events and Adventures Company, for singles seeking new friends and adventure in the Midwest and abroad, needed a tour company. Leisurely, he made his way toward the coffee kiosk, since the doors wouldn't open for another twenty minutes. He felt confident in finding the perfect tour company for his company's travel needs today, if his gut feeling was accurate and it usually was.

Finally, when the doors opened for the Expo, Tristan walked up to the counter and greeted Holly. "Hi, I think this might be exactly what I'm looking for." He picked up a brochure which oddly looked familiar.

"Well, that would make my job easier." Holly laughed.

"What can Nordic Travel and Tours do for you and your company?"

"My company is Minnesota Events and Adventures for singles. We set up events and travel destinations for our members. I'm looking for a company that can set up the tours and travel parts for us to sell as a group package to our clients. Basically, my company gets the people and your company would set everything up."

"This could be a perfect match because what we do is all the planning for trips such as the air, hotels, transportation and tours."

Tristan picked up a business card from the counter. "Are you Annika?"

"No, I'm Holly. Annika Karlstad is the owner and manager of the company and I'm her assistant." She pulled out her IPad with Annika's calendar. "I think you'd probably like to talk to her in person, so she can go over everything in detail. I have her calendar up on my IPad, so I'd be happy to set up an appointment next week for you."

Tristan pulled out his phone from his pocket and brought up his calendar. "Would Tuesday work?"

"She has a ten o'clock slot open."

"That should work." He pulled out his business card and handed it to Holly. "My name is Tristan Torgersen and I look forward to meeting Ms. Karlstad."

Holly smiled as she watched Tristan move on down the aisle past the rows of vendors.

Annika regretted not bringing a lunch when she saw the prices and the menu. Not that she had much choice at this point, so she ordered a salad and ice tea. While she waited for her food she checked her phone for any messages.

"So we meet again."

She turned to see who spoke. It was the man she'd literally run into earlier. "Hello. Again."

"How is the rest of your day going?"

"Much better. How about you?" Annika asked.

"Already made it half way through the auditorium. I think I've already found what I was looking for though."

"Oh, so will you still walk through the other half?"

"I'm here, so might as well take a look in case some other company strikes my fancy." Tristan chuckled.

"Well, best of luck...I guess I never got your name."

"Tristan."

"Well then Tristan, I'm Annika. Hope you find what you're looking for at the Travel Expo."

"I think I already may have found exactly what I'm looking for, Annika." Tristan smiled.

Annika heard her number called. "That's me. It's been nice running into you again." She gave him her best smile, then walked up to the counter to pick up her food. Discreetly, she positioned herself, so she could see if he'd left.

Tristan caught her eyes drifting his direction and tipped his head slightly in a nod, turned and walked back into the auditorium.

Why she felt so flustered around this guy, she had no idea. Her heart was racing and she knew she wanted to see him again. She knew nothing about him, so it was utterly ridiculous to be feeling this way. Besides, she wasn't looking for someone to date. At least not this year anyway, because she needed to stay focused on her company. She was personally responsible for making it a success. She didn't need any distractions.

After she'd finished eating her lunch, she made her way down a couple of aisles to check out the competition before going back to her booth. She felt confident about her company and what they had to offer clients. They offered bus tours to events and destinations in Minnesota and even some to the neighboring states of Wisconsin, Iowa, South Dakota and North Dakota. The tours to Scandinavia had always been top rated by their customers because they were unique in offering many off the beaten path options which were sought after by those with Scandinavian ancestry.

"Did I miss anything?" Annika asked taking a seat next to Holly.

"I put a couple of appointments on your calendar for next week that I think might be great new clients and handed out quite a few of the brochures."

"Tell me about the appointments."

"One is for a company looking to book some flight packages for their sales people who made their goals. And one is for the local company, Minnesota Events and Adventures. The company is for singles and they book group travel in and out of Minnesota for their events."

"Good job, Holly. Those sound like they have great potential for us."

A group of young people walked up to the table to ask about the trips to Iceland. Annika eagerly became engaged in conversation revolving around her passion for travel to the Scandinavian countries.

www.ingramcontent.com/pod-product-compliance
Lightning Source LLC
Chambersburg PA
CBHW022053170626
46808CB00003B/1457